The Road
An Allegory

Gerald Thompson

Finger Lakes Publishing

LIMA, NY

Gerald Thompson / Finger Lakes Publishing
1854 Eastwood Dr
Lima, NY 14485
www.fingerlakespublishing.net

Publisher's Note: This is a work of fiction. Names, characters, places, and incidents are a product of the author's imagination. Locales and public names are sometimes used for atmospheric purposes. Any resemblance to actual people, living or dead, or to businesses, companies, events, institutions, or locales is completely coincidental.

Book Layout © 2021 BookDesignTemplates.com

The Road: an Allegory / Gerald Thompson. -- 1st ed.
ISBN 978-1-7359287-5-3

"Enter through the narrow gate. For wide is the gate, and broad is the Road that leads to Destruction, and many enter through it. But small is the gate and narrow the Road that leads to life, and only a few find it.

Matthew 7:13-14. (NIV)

The Road

"Let me help ya up, Laddie," said the stranger. Two strong hands grabbed me on each side of my bicep and yanked me to my feet. I took a step and stumbled again. The strong hands held me up a second time.

"C'mon, we've got to keep moving, or we're both goners."

Dazed, I mumbled, "Thanks."

"Quite the bump ya got there."

My head ached. I reached up and gingerly touched the growing goose egg on my forehead. "Did you see what happened?"

"Aye, a hole opened at your feet. You didn't see it. You tripped on the edge and nearly fell into it. If you fell in, you'd be gone for good. Instead, you fell on the Road, bumped your head, and were about to be trampled. I had a chance, so I nabbed ya. Many fall, but few help them up."

"Thanks for grabbing me," I said. I stuck out my hand, "My name is Chris."

"I'm Fingal," he said, shaking my hand. "Have you been on the Road long?"

"Eighteen years. I turned eighteen two months ago, but I lost my parents when the flow slowed, and everybody jammed together about a month ago. In all the jostling and pushing, we got separated. I've been looking for them since."

"I've been on the Road for some twenty-eight years. An' being separated from loved ones on the Road is common. But fear not Laddie; we shall walk together for a while and help each other."

The Road.

I think a lot about the Road. *Why is it here? Why are we on it?*

The Road is wide. I can barely make out the far side when I stand on edge. Everybody walks it. It's smooth and asphalt gray, with a bit of loose debris swirling about. The Road is flat at a level from side to side, front to back.

The Road is comfortable. The bright Sun warms my face, and the gentle Breeze cools my brow.

The Road offers companionship. I've had some great friends, and we traveled together until the ebb and flow of the people separated us.

The Road is full of people traveling in the same direction. The mass of humanity is like a stream. Sometimes, it is slow and calm, and sometimes there are rapids. Everybody bunches together periodically; other times, there's breathing space between groups or individuals.

Most folks treat each other well except when someone falls. The human river cannot stop. Standing against the flow of humanity to help someone up is difficult and dangerous. The odds of the Good Samaritan also being trampled are high. I'm fortunate that Fingal grabbed me.

I've often wondered about the Road. *Who made it?* You can see a long way. It is as straight as an arrow. Trees or thickets obscure what lies beyond the edges, and Mountains soar above each side. Sometimes, there would be a break between the trunks, and I could peer beyond the Road for a moment before the mass of humanity pushed me on.

My eyes were drawn to the Mountains. But I thought only an idiot would leave the comfort and relative safety of the Road. I've seen a few people strike off into the tangle of bushes. Once in a while, I'd spot small groups high up in the Mountains, which looked impossible to climb. Still, I wondered what's up there.

I turned to my companion. "Fingal, what's in the Wilds and the Mountains that line the Road?"

"I don't know, Laddie. Some say there are animals that eat ya, and others say monsters live in it. I don't understand the attraction to go and find out."

His answer didn't quench my curiosity. I sidled towards the green wall along the edge of the Road. *What lies beyond?* I reached for the delicate leaves when a hand knocked my arm down.

"What are ya doing, Laddie? Some say it's death to touch those leaves. Why take the chance?"

"I don't know. It's strange, the Mountains, the Wilds, they call to me."

"Come on, we best be movin' or be trampled."

I kept glancing sideways at the thicket along the Road and the Mountains that rose beyond. Fingal's right: it's stupid to leave the ease of the Road.

A few days later, I spied someone by the edge of the Road. *Is that a break in the thicket?* A woman called to the passing crowd. As we approached, her voice got louder.

"At the end of the Road is Destruction and pain! Leave it while you can! There's life in the Wilds! Come join me. Save yourselves."

"Fingal, what do you make of her?"

"Nut job. I've seen quite a few. Standing, sitting, or darting into the Road, trying to grab or convince you to run off into the Wild with them. Claimin' Destruction, whatever that is, is at the Road's end."

"Could they be right?"

"Laddie, the Road is way easier than the Wilds. It seems you'd be swallowed up out there faster than here. Besides, who'd put Destruction at the end of the Road? Makes no sense."

The woman's voice faded as we passed. I stole one last look over my shoulder. She had a hold of someone's arm. The man pushed, and she fell back into the thicket.

Crazy, yet I still had an itch in my brain to go to the Mountains.

****

Time passed, a year perhaps, and the itch in my brain lessened but never went away. My companion, Fingal, still traveled the Road with me. We had lively discussions sprinkled with laughter.

One day, Fingal said something funny. I laughed so hard that I didn't see the woman stop in the Road.

I nearly plowed into her while she stood staring at the Mountains.

"Lady, get moving or be trampled."

"I'm a-movin'; I'm a-movin.' But man, look at the Mountains. I can hear them calling me. I wonder what's up there."

"I don't know. The Mountains have called me, too. Thankfully, their cry is faint when I focus on the Road."

"Hmm, too bad. My name's Chineka, what's yours?"
"My name is Chris, and this is Fingal."
"Please to meet ya, Chris, Fingal.

"Hello, Lassie. How about you walk with us for a while?"
"Thanks, I think I will."

Chineka was a hoot. She energized our conversations, but she talked almost non-stop. Our talks wove a winding path through every known topic, but each discussion seemed to circle back to Wilds or the Mountains and the secrets they held. She'd get excited and was ready to charge into the Wilds. More than once, we had to turn her attention back to the Road.

But the more we talked about the Wilds and the Mountains, the more I thought about them. Occasionally, Chineka dared me to break through the barrier with her and see what hid behind the green wall.

One day, Fingal became angry and left us. He yelled that he was sick and tired of listening to us and went looking for someone who spoke sense instead of nonsense. I grieved at Fingal's departure. I walked in silence, lost in thought.

"Chris, look. There's a break in the ticket, and someone's standing in it."

I could make out a man's head above the crowd before us. As we got closer to him, we heard him shouting.

"The Road leads only to Destruction! Please, I'm begging you, get off the Road!" A man ahead of us spat on him. The stranger wiped the spit from his face as we drew next to him.

Chineka pulled me into the opening and out of the flow of humanity. "Let's see what's in the wild, Chris."

"I-I don't know." I turned to the stranger. "Hey, how'd you know the Road leads to Destruction?"

"I've seen it. Just follow the Path, and you'll see it too."

I looked into the brush and the Path that tunneled through it. Sharp thorns decorated the branches. I hesitated and looked back at the Road. Cool, comfortable, and familiar, everything I knew was there.

But I couldn't ignore the call of the Mountains any longer. I wanted to know the secrets they held. I looked at Chineka and gave a nod.

With a cry of delight, she grabbed my hand and pulled me down the narrow Path. The man by the Road whooped and celebrated as we disappeared from sight.

We wound our way around and through the vegetation for a long time. The thick air was hot and oppressive, and my clothes were drenched in sweat. The Road was never like this, and my mind filled with doubt.

"Chineka, this is stupid. I'm hot and tired and want to return to the Road."

"Don't be dumb, Chris. The Road is boring. This is exciting. I am going on. Will ya give it one more day?"

"One more day," I grumbled.

Many other Paths crossed ours. Some seemed to turn towards the Road, while others led to the Mountains. Chineka was determined to reach the Mountains. Walking became more challenging as the Path climbed. Soon, we broke into the Sunlight and cool Breezes at the foot of the Mountains.

Refreshed, I looked up. From a distance, the Mountains were daunting. Up close, the steep sides and rock outcropping terrified me. *How are we to get up that?*

"Ain't it beautiful, Chris?"

"No, it's not. There's no way up. It's impossible!

"We can do it, Chris! Wait . . . Who is that?"

I followed Chineka's gaze up the Mountain. Shading my eyes from the Sun, I saw a man who must have been part mountain goat. He jumped from ledge to ledge and bounced down the steep slope until he stopped about six feet from us.

"Greetings," he called.

"Greetings," Chineka and I replied in harmony.

"Who are you?" I asked.

"My name and function are the same. You can call me the Guide. I'm here to help you up the Mountains. The Path is narrow and steep. You couldn't make it without me."

"The Guide, Nice to meet you. Lead the way," said Chineka.

With that, the Guide turned and started up the Mountain. He was right; we'd never make it on our own. He directed our hands and feet as we climbed. Even though the Path was steep and the rocks dangerous, I felt no fear. We didn't talk much. We needed to concentrate on the Path. We climbed for hours.

"Almost there," the Guide called down. "We'll rest on the next ledge."

I pulled myself up onto the ledge. For a minute, I just lay there, eyes closed, recovering from our exertions and enjoying the Sun and Breeze.

"Would ya look at that?" Chineka whispered in awe.

I sat up and looked out. The high altitude made my head spin, so I closed my eyes momentarily. When I opened them again, I felt like I was atop the world.

High above us, the Sun shone through wispy clouds. Across the wide valley, another mountain range mirrored ours. Far below ran the Road. It looked just as straight from the Mountains as it did below. The humanity that flowed along the Road looked even more like water.

"What's that?" I pointed at the Road below. Two large holes opened, several people fell in, and they closed.

"That's Destruction," the Guide said. "They're holes that open randomly, and anyone traveling the Road can fall in. Destruction is found only on the Road."

"What's in the holes?"

"An eternity of darkness and pain," the Guide sadly replied.

We rested and watched the Road, especially the holes when they appeared. Sometimes, they swallowed no one; other times, they devoured one or two souls. One person tripped on the edge, and the flow of humanity trampled them. *That could've happened to me. Thank you, Fingal.*

The Guide stood and spoke. "We're almost to the summit. The Path will be much easier there."

As we stood, Chineka screamed as she disappeared over the cliff. I raced to the edge and watched her fall into the trees far below.

"Ch-Ch-Chinneekkaaaa! . . . Oh, Chineka," I sobbed.

"Friend, why do you cry?" asked the Guide.

I stood and yelled in his face, "Chineka's gone, destroyed!"

"Chineka is gone, but she is not destroyed. I told you Destruction only comes to those on the Road. She may be bruised and battered, but she'll find the Guide and climb the Mountains again." The Guide turned and followed the Path. Relieved, I dried my tears and followed him.

Soon, we were on the summit. The Path clearly followed the ridge of the Mountains.

Years passed, and the beautiful peaks and alpine valleys were a joy to climb. Sometimes, the Path meandered a bit but always followed the Sun. Often, I'd look below to the Road where Destruction lay hidden, and my heart cried every time someone disappeared into a hole.

"What's happening to the Road?"

"This is where the Road narrows. The people pack together, becoming a solid mass of humanity. Look over there," the Guide pointed to the enormous gate below?"

"Yes."

"Just past the gate, the Road becomes steep and slippery. Soon, the people will fall and slide down the slope into a giant hole. Destruction. There, they will suffer for all time."

"But that's not fair!" I cried.

"The Sun shines on all, the Breeze refreshes all, and the Mountains call to all. Many hear, but only a few follow the voice of the Mountains. Witnesses line the Road, and there are Guides stationed throughout the Mountains to lead people up the Path to the narrow gate. We're almost at the gate. Do you see it yonder?" the Guide said.

Looking ahead, I saw a wall about eight feet high, in which was a gate about seven feet tall and two feet wide.

Beyond the wall rose a large mountain into the sky, and on its sides stood a great city bathed in radiant Sunlight. The golden light lit up pearlescent spires. A wide, gently sloped apron of green grass and trees lay below the city. I could see people walking on it. Birds fluttered about, and children and animals played together. Peace and joy shimmered in the air.

I smiled and hurried down the Path, ready to pass through the gate, the Guide running behind me to catch up.

I stopped just short of the gate. My head turned, and I looked down at Destruction at the end of the Road.

"If I pass through the gate, will I be allowed to return?"

"No," replied the Guide.

"Do I have to go through the gate now?

"No," replied the Guide.

"May I go and try to warn the people and direct them to the Path?"

"Yes, for a time," smiled the Guide.

I turned and jumped down the Mountain to the Road.

"Enter through the narrow gate. For wide is the gate, and broad is the Road that leads to Destruction, and many enter through it. But small is the gate and narrow the Road that leads to life, and only a few find it.

Matthew 7:13-14. (NIV)

Character's Names

Chris: Short for Christopher, "Bearing Christ inside."
Fingal: Scottish for "White Stranger."
Chineka: African for "God Listens."

Notes

Notes

Discussion Questions

Being an allegory, almost everything in the story is a metaphor for something else. Discuss each of the story elements listed and how they relate to real life, especially how they relate to your life.

The Road:

The Sun:

The Mountains:

The Mountains call to all, but not all listen:

The Wilds at the foot of the Mountains:

The Guide:

Chineka's Fall:

Why wasn't the Guide concerned about Chineka after the fall:

The relative ease of walking along the peaks:

The Great City:

Destruction:

Answer Key

Most of the allegory is straightforward and not meant to be too deep, but I will point out a couple of things. The discussion and the relevance to each of us are more important than the details of a story. Not everyone's answer will be the same.

The Road is life and the time allotted to each of us. It's comfortable and easy to go through life without considering the journey's destination.

The Sun is Jesus.

The Mountains are God's Word, calling to all of humanity. Many hear them, but sadly, few act.

The Wilds are when you realize that following God is not easy; you must persevere through trials to mature in your faith and reap God's blessings.

The Guide is the Holy Spirit, guiding us through our life.

Chineka's fall represents the times we have fallen in our faith. Fortunately, God does not send us to Destruction when we get tripped up.

As you mature in your faith, there are few doubts. You follow God, and while the Path is not always straight, you know the destination and that God intends only the best for you.

The Great City: Heaven

Destruction: Hell

One Sunday many years ago, The pastor preached about the wide and narrow gates from Matthew 7: 13-14. God planted the idea for the Road. The idea plagued me, and I could not get it out of my head. Only after I put the Road to paper did it leave my mind.

This illustrated version of *The Road: an Allegory* is perfect for yourself, to be given away, a gift for new Christians, or a single/filler lesson and discussion for a small group. Volume discounts are available.

To order additional copies, go to theroadallegory.com.

God also inspired me to write **Demons and Dreams** and its sequel, **Demons and Angels**. *Demons and Dreams* is based on an actual nightmare I had. Both books are Christian thrillers, like books written by Frank Peretti and Ted Dekker.

Find out more at fingerlakespublishing.net

****